Hanging out at Charlotte's posh house

The English Roses

A Rose by Any Other Name

CALLAWAY ARTS & ENTERTAINMENT
19 FULTON STREET, FIFTH FLOOR, NEW YORK, NEW YORK 10038

PUFFIN BOOKS
Published by the Penguin Group
Penguin Young Readers Group, 345 Hudson Street, New York, New York 10014, U.S.A.
Penguin Group (Canada), 90 Eglinton Avenue East, Suite 700, Toronto, Ontario,
Canada M4P 2Y3 (a division of Pearson Penguin Canada Inc.)

Penguin Books Ltd., Registered Offices: 80 Strand, London WC2R 0RL, England

First published in the United States of America by Callaway Arts & Entertainment and Puffin Books, 2007

1   3   5   7   9   10   8   6   4   2

First Edition

Produced by Callaway Arts & Entertainment
Nicholas Callaway, President and Publisher
Cathy Ferrara, Managing Editor and Production Director
Toshiya Masuda, Art Director • Nelson Gómez, Director of Digital Technology
Joya Rajadhyaksha, Editor • Amy Cloud, Editor
Ivan Wong, Jr. and José Rodríguez, Production
Kathryn Bradwell, Executive Assistant to the Publisher

Special thanks to Doug Whiteman and Mariann Donato.

Library of Congress Cataloging-in-Publication Data is available.

Puffin Books ISBN 978-0-14-240885-8

Printed in the United States of America

www.madonna.com   www.callaway.com   www.penguin.com/youngreaders

All of Madonna's proceeds from this book will be donated to
Raising Malawi (www.raisingmalawi.org), an orphan-care initiative.

Contents

CHAPTER I

Charlotte's Best Day Ever

You have surely heard of the English Roses by now. If not, you must be talking on the phone twenty-four/seven, or spending all your time mooning over crushes, or simply walking around wearing earmuffs and a blindfold at all times. Which, if you ask me, isn't a good idea for any reason. Not to mention you are *really* missing out by not knowing the English Roses. The English Roses are *not* to be missed!

The English Roses are five best-of-the-best friends: Charlotte Ginsberg, Binah Rossi, Grace Harrison, Amy Brook, and Nicole Rissman. Most people are lucky to find just one best friend; the English Roses were each four times as lucky! Which, I don't think I have to tell you, is very lucky indeed.

Have you ever had a Best Day? Not just a good day; everyone has good days. A *Best Day*. A day when you can feel the sun shining even *before* you wake up. When you can't stop thinking about blueberry-pistachio pancakes with butterscotch sauce on the

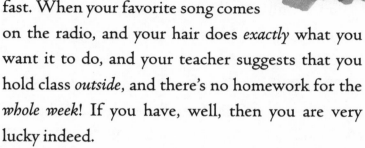

side, and it just so happens that's *exactly* what's on the table for breakfast. When your favorite song comes on the radio, and your hair does *exactly* what you want it to do, and your teacher suggests that you hold class *outside*, and there's no homework for the *whole week*! If you have, well, then you are very lucky indeed.

And so is Charlotte, for that is exactly what she felt when she woke up one fine, sunny, unseasonably warm autumn morning. It was going to be a Best Day; she could feel it in the air.

"Good morning, Gracie!" Charlotte beamed, rushing out the door to meet her friend, who had been pitching tiny pebbles at her bedroom window. She did a twirl, and her pink silk dress billowed in the breeze.

Grace smiled and turned down the volume on her ever-present MP3 player. Hey, a girl's got to have her accessories!

"Think fast!" Grace said, and tossed a ball at Charlotte. Her frilly friend squealed and ducked. Grace giggled. "Gotcha! C'mon. Don't you think I know by now you're allergic to sports?"

Charlotte smiled. "That doesn't mean I can't beat you to Amy's. Last one there's a . . . dirty gym sock!" And with that, Charlotte took off—new dress, pink bows in her silky black hair, satin ballet flats, and all.

"Hey, no fair!" Grace took off after her, kicking her ball as she ran.

The English Roses had been walking to school together since forever. Well, Binah had only joined them last year, but it felt as if they'd known one another all their lives. By the time Grace and Charlotte picked up Amy, then Nicole, finally Binah, and arrived at Hampstead School, they were more out of breath from giggle fits than from the walk itself. That's the way it is with best friends. Now just imagine having *four* of them! There was never a shortage of things to talk about or laugh about and certainly to gossip about. And today was no exception. *Today*, thought Charlotte, *is shaping up to be a perfectly perfect day.*

CHAPTER 2

Sorry, Charlie!

the "sixth grade" building

←

The morning, unfortunately, was uneventful. But as the five friends shuffled back from lunch, they heard a familiar voice behind them.

"Hello, girls!" exclaimed their beloved teacher from last year, Miss Fluffernutter. Miss Fluffernutter's favorite accessory, besides her

extremely fluffy hair, was always an armful of what looked like the inside of a very full filing cabinet. And today was no exception.

"Good afternoon, Miss Fluffernutter," the English Roses chorused back.

Miss Fluffernutter beamed. "It is going to be a very good afternoon indeed! Now quick—off to class! I'll be visiting later, and I have some extremely excellent news!"

The girls took their seats in Mrs. Moss's classroom. They liked Mrs. Moss, though she was pretty

much the exact opposite of Miss Fluffernutter. Her desk was always spotless. She always wore neatly pressed pantsuits with matching silk scarves knotted loosely around her neck. And her hair was remarkably flat!

As the class settled in, Charlotte straightened her dress, crossed her legs, and felt a very familiar *tug* on her hair. She whipped around.

Sure enough, there was William Worthington, smirking his signature smirk. Eyebrows arched over his flashing blue-green eyes, he stared at Charlotte as if *she* was the one who'd pulled *his* hair. The nerve!

You probably have a William Worthington of your own in your life. If not, you've surely met one. William Worthingtons are always there to untie your hair ribbons, scrawl scribbles on your notes, and get you into trouble for talking in class. William Worthingtons are impossible to talk to but equally impossible to ignore. And the most frustrating part of all is the fact that William Worthingtons are just so insufferably *cute*.

"Hello, Charlie," said William Worthington.

Charlotte glared at him and smoothed her hair. "Hello yourself. And I told you: only my *friends* call me Charlie." Charlotte gave her raven hair a toss and turned back to the front of the room.

"Sorry, Charlie." William leaned in and gave her hair another tug. "I thought we *were* friends!"

Charlotte stared straight ahead. She was not going to participate in William's shenanigans today. Not when Miss Fluffernutter was coming with "extremely excellent" news to relay.

"Aw, c'mon, Charlie. Don't be mad. I'm just playin'." Charlotte focused on her pearl pink manicure.

"Forgive me, Charlie. I swear, Charlie, I'll never call you Charlie again." If there's one thing William Worthingtons are, it's persistent!

Charlotte turned around in a huff and met his eyes. "You can call me whatever you want if you'll just *stop talking!*"

"Charlotte, your attention, please," Mrs. Moss chastised from the front of the room. Charlotte sighed. He'd gotten her again. William smiled his infuriatingly irresistible smile. "Sorry," he mouthed. And *winked*! Charlotte shook her head.

"I do apologize, Mrs. Moss. It won't happen again." *Until tomorrow*, she thought. That William Worthington! Amy, Grace, Nicole, and Binah sent Charlotte sympathetic looks.

Mrs. Moss cleared her throat. "Now then. We have a special guest. Miss Fluffernutter is here with an important announcement."

Miss Fluffernutter bustled to the front of the classroom. "As you all know, as sixth graders you are the eldest at Hampstead. You 'rule the school,' as the homies say!" The class tittered.

"Well, as sixth graders," Miss Fluffernutter continued, "you have a special privilege. I am pleased to announce the annual sixth-grade play: *Romeo and Juliet: The Musical!*" The entire class murmured excitedly. The sixth-grade play was the event of the season. The whole school came to watch, and parents were invited. The English Roses could barely contain their excitement. They looked at one another across the room and could not wait for class to end. When girls need to talk, they need to talk!

CHAPTER 3

M.O.U.I.

No sooner had the final bell rung than the English Roses were off to Charlotte's house as fast as their legs could carry them. Charlotte's was the unofficial headquarters for M.O.U.I.: Meetings of Utmost Importance. And if you ever saw Charlotte's house, you'd understand why!

"Good afternoon, Miss Charlotte." Her butler, Winston, stood at the base of the drive. He handed each girl a pink sparkly drink in a long-stemmed glass. "Strawberry spritzers for the misses."

"Thank you, Winston!" chorused the girls.

The girls bounded up the stairs and into Charlotte's room. Winston followed with a silver tray heaped with goodies Charlotte's chef, Nigella, had prepared: mini peanut-butter-and-jam sandwiches (with the crusts cut off, of course), apple wedges with caramel dipping sauce, licorice bites, and crackers spread with creamy cheese.

The girls fell upon the treat tray in a flurry, but snacking was the last thing on Charlotte's mind. She

sandwiches...

clapped her hands. "M.O.U.I. is called to order, ladies!" Munching quietly, Amy, Nicole, Binah, and Grace shared a look. Charlotte had been talking about the sixth-grade play since . . . well . . . since *forever*. She was going to be a famous actress-slash-singer-slash-socialite, after all. For as long as they could remember, she'd been counting down the years, then months, then *days* until this very event.

"First order of business," Charlotte said. "Who wants to do what?"

Amy raised her hand. "I'd love to help with the costumes!" The girls immediately exclaimed in agreement.

Charlotte smiled. "I cannot wait to wear your designs, Amy."

Amy grinned, twiddling a lock of bright red hair around her finger. "Thanks, guys!" She flopped back into the pink fluff of Charlotte's huge, glorious bed, visions of fabulous fabrics dancing in her head.

"Okay. Next?" Charlotte looked around the room. "Binah? What about you?"

"Oh, I don't know," said Binah. "I don't think theater is for me."

Charlotte shook her head emphatically. "Nonsense. The theater is for *everyone*. You just haven't found your calling yet." She paused for a moment, then had it. "Set designer! It's perfect. You're a magnificent artist, Binah."

Binah shook her head. "No—"

"Yes!" cried the girls. Binah really was quite good. She'd even painted gorgeous portraits of each of her friends. Charlotte pointed to her wall, where her own likeness hung in a sparkling crystal frame.

CHARLOTTE by BINAH

"Emma says it looks *exactly* like me."

Binah swallowed the glee that bubbled up inside her. Emma was Charlotte's older sister. She was stunning and sweet . . . and in *high school.* If Emma liked your drawing, your drawing was *good*!

"Okay, okay!" Binah laughed. "If Miss Fluffernutter will let me do it."

Charlotte smiled, pleased. "She's sure to do just that. Alrighty then. Nicole? What about you?"

Nicole looked up from the notes she was diligently scribbling in her trusty notebook.

Charlotte held up a hand. "Wait—I know the perfect thing. Stage manager, of course!"

Nicole smiled. She'd been secretly hoping for that position. "Well, if you think I'd be any good . . ."

Amy bounced up. "Would you *ever*! You were *born* for it, Nikki!" Binah, Grace, and Charlotte agreed.

"You get to boss people around," said Grace. "You know you can't say no to that!" The girls laughed. They often said they'd never make it through the day without Nicole. She always reminded them when their homework was due or when they had a quiz coming up, she never once forgot a birthday, and she was always willing to

share her perfectly perfect notes. Doesn't everyone wish they had a best friend like that?

Nicole marked the breaking news in her notebook: "Possible stage manager: Nicole."

"Fabulous," said Charlotte. "Now that just leaves Grace."

The girls turned to look at Grace, sitting cross-legged on the carpet. She had a tower of tiny sandwiches balanced on the plate in front of her like a house of cards. She concentrated intensely, biting the corner off a peanut-butter-and-jam petit four so it would fit right . . . on . . . top . . . and . . .

"Ahem!" Charlotte's hand swooped in and pulled a sticky square right out from under Grace's tower. The whole thing toppled into her lap, and she looked up sheepishly.

"What have I told you about playing with your food, Grace? I swear, it must have been Opposite Day when they named you."

Grace's eyes narrowed, but she swallowed her response and popped a peanut-butter square into her mouth.

"Carn't talk—mowf full!"

Charlotte sighed and shook her head. "Okay, Grace. When you've *swallowed*, please tell us what job you want in the sixth-grade play."

Grace gulped. "Um . . . audience member!" The girls giggled. "Seriously, Charlie," Grace continued, "this is your thing. Your mom was Juliet in her sixth-grade play. Emma was Juliet in hers. My job will be to sit in the front row and say 'Break a leg,' and throw flowers on the stage and yell 'Bravo!' I'm not cut out for the whole drama thing. Besides, football season's coming up. I've gotta practice." (Football: what silly Americans call soccer.) Charlotte started to object, but Grace stood up. "In fact, I should be getting home. My brothers said they'd practice with me tonight. If I'm late they'll make me clean their cleats!" She gathered up her back-pack and bounded to the door.

did you get a good look @ Charlie's MUM?

she's sooooo COOL!

"You don't know what you're missing!" Charlotte called after her. Nicole closed her notebook, already imagining the binder with little flags she'd make that night. Amy bounced excitedly, flipping through a fashion magazine for inspiration. Binah couldn't wait to get home to tell her dad about her possible new job as set designer!

Charlotte turned around to catch a glimpse of herself in the mirror. She stood up straight and did a small curtsy. She was going to make the best Juliet the world had ever seen!

A lovely lunch is almost ruined!

CHAPTER 4

Some People Just Don't Appreciate the Arts

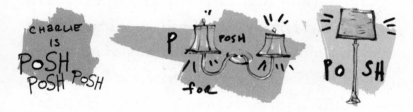

Whenever the sun was shining, the English Roses ate lunch in the same spot. As soon as the bell rang, they sprinted to a patch of exceptionally soft grass behind the school.

On this particular day, the sun was shining and a light breeze tickled the leaves that were just beginning to change color. Charlotte opened her lunch box and took out some cucumber sandwiches.

Binah unwrapped her brown bag lunch to find a tuna salad sandwich and a note from her father. "To my favorite future set designer. Hope you have a great day! Love, Papa." Binah smiled and folded the note into a tiny square, then zipped it into her schoolbag. She had a whole drawer at home filled with daily lunch notes from her father. He hadn't skipped a day yet!

Amy and Grace opened their bags. "What'cha got?" Grace asked. Amy looked down and made a face. "Leftover meatloaf. You?" Grace looked at her own and made a gagging gesture. "Macaroni salad." They looked at each other. "Switch!" Grace and Amy almost always liked each other's lunches better than their own. It was practically guaranteed.

Nicole was the only one of the English Roses who bought a school lunch. She just loved the way everything was divided into its own section of the tray. Nicole absolutely hated it when different parts of a meal touched each other. If her peas got too close to her chicken salad, she simply couldn't eat it!

Charlotte talked a mile a minute. "Emma stayed up until ten o'clock going over my monologue with me," she babbled. "She says my memorization and posture are even better than hers when she was my age. I mean, I don't believe that, but still—"

"HEADS UP!" Before the Roses could even blink, the looming shadow of an incoming ball cast its pall over their picnic. Charlotte shrieked and flung her hands over her head. The ball came speeding toward them, disaster approaching, when "*Oof!*" Charlotte peeked out from between her fingers just in time to see Grace leap up and deflect the ball with her *forehead*. She breathed a sigh of relief until she heard an irritatingly familiar voice behind her.

"Whoa! Nice one, Harrison!"

Grace kicked up the ball and juggled it from knee to knee. "Yeah, well, looks like you could use a lesson or two, Worthington." She kicked the ball high in the air and "headed" it over to William, who caught it. "See?" said Grace with a laugh. "Lesson one: no hands."

William dropped the ball and kicked it back over to his buddies on the field. "You got me. Say, you wanna play? We're down one, and there's still half an hour before class."

Grace grinned. "Sure—if you can handle getting beat by a *girl*!"

"Yeah, right." William laughed. "We'll see about that." He turned to Charlotte. "How 'bout you, Charlie? Wanna play?"

Grace stifled a giggle. Picturing Charlotte playing sports was just about the funniest thing she could think of.

"No thank you," said Charlotte primly.

William just smiled. "Whatever you say, Charlie. Wouldn't want you to break a nail." And before Charlotte could retort, he was jogging away with a wink.

Grace shrugged. What is there to do about a

William Worthington, anyway? "Bye, guys. See you later!" And with that, she was down on the field.

So it was only four English Roses who walked

into school as the back-to-class bell rang. Miss Fluffernutter was in the hallway, posting a large sheet of paper up on the wall. She caught sight of the girls and broke into a delighted smile.

"Why, hello, ladies! You're just in time! Here is the sign-up sheet for the sixth-grade play auditions. Who's in?"

Charlotte sprinted over and grabbed the pen from her teacher's hand. "I most certainly am! She reached up to the tippy-top of the list and signed her name with a flourish. "There!"

"Can I help with costumes, Miss Fluffernutter? I have some fabulous ideas already. I've drawn up some sketches . . ." Amy opened a large sketchbook filled with brightly colored patterns and swatches of exotic fabrics.

"Ooh! How delightful, Amy!" Miss Fluffernutter exclaimed. "Why, I can think of no one better to fill that role."

Binah raised her hand shyly. "I'd like to work on the sets," she said. Miss Fluffernutter clapped her hands.

"Splendid! You shall do just that."

"Ahem." Nicole had straightened the list so it was now at a perfect ninety-degree angle with the floor. "I can be the stage manager. I have a rehearsal schedule all mapped out—"

Miss Fluffernutter chimed in before she could finish: "Nicole, you've got the job. I certainly couldn't do it without you!"

The girls smiled at their delightfully discombobulated teacher. "Well, off to class," said Nicole.

"We don't want to be late!" added Charlotte.

"Wait!" Miss Fluffernutter cried. The girls stopped in their tracks. "I only count *four* English Roses! Wherever is Grace?"

Charlotte waved dismissively. "Oh, she's off sporting with the boys, as usual." She shrugged. "Some people just don't appreciate the arts!"

CHAPTER 5

Last Call for Auditions

The next morning, Hampstead was positively buzzing with energy. It seemed as if no one could concentrate—not even Mrs. Moss!

Grace, however, was as cool as a cucumber. And she didn't seem to mind at all being the only Rose not participating in the sixth-grade play. Whenever someone asked her why she wasn't involved, Charlotte would jump in and explain for her. "Grace would rather kick a ball around all day." And Grace would nod, rolling her eyes as she popped in her headphones and juggled a football in time to her music.

Finally, after what felt like an eternity—no, an eternity of eternities!—the last bell rang. The English Roses filtered into the auditorium along with the rest of the school. Not everyone was auditioning for a role in the sixth-grade play, but everyone wanted to see who was!

Miss Fluffernutter sat in the front row, her glasses perched on the tip of her nose and her hair so fluffy, it was lucky no one was sitting behind her! Nicole took a seat next to her, notebook and pencil in hand. A murmur rolled through the crowd as the students settled in. Nicole handed the audition list to Miss Fluffernutter, and they were ready to begin.

It seemed as if every single sixth grader wanted to be part of the play. Everyone who was anyone auditioned, from Fritz Flotterdam to the twins, Taffy and Tricky Ferguson. Miss Fluffernutter complimented each student after his or her performance, and during the entire time, Nicole's head was bent over her notebook, scribbling furiously.

Finally Miss Fluffernutter looked up from her notes. "Next: Charlotte Ginsberg!" Charlotte sprang to her feet.

"Go, Charlie!" Grace shouted from the back of the auditorium. Amy blew her a kiss, and Binah waved. Nicole sent an encouraging smile from her seat next to Miss Fluffernutter.

Charlotte took the stage and looked out at the crowd. The smiling faces staring back at her seemed to send her energy that went coursing through her veins. She felt positively electric. She took a deep breath, and the words she'd been rehearsing over and over and over again just came pouring out. Charlotte almost forgot where she was; in that moment, she truly felt she *was* Juliet.

When she finished, the crowd erupted in applause. The English Roses cheered wildly. Charlotte's heart was beating so fast she felt the whole room must be able to hear it.

Nicole wrote down: "Bravo!"

Miss Fluffernutter called for everyone to settle down. "Simply wonderful, Charlotte." She consulted her list. "Alrighty then! Next up, William Worthington." Charlotte started. William Worthington, *auditioning?*

"Nice job, Charlie," William leaned over and whispered in her ear as he passed her. He gave her hair a quick tug. "Maybe you'll be my Juliet!"

Charlotte stood, frozen, unable to formulate a response. She blushed and nodded—*nodded!*—before running off the stage and into the arms of her waiting friends.

The rest of the tryouts were a blur. William Worthington's audition garnered a "Wow" in Nicole's notebook. Charlotte sat in the back of the auditorium, trying to concentrate on the other auditions. But she couldn't stop one single phrase from running over and over again through her head: *Maybe you'll be my Juliet.* She felt warm and glanced around guiltily, as if someone might be able to overhear her thoughts. Imagine, William a Romeo to her Juliet. She couldn't figure out why the idea had her in such a tizzy.

It was after dark when the auditions finally

ended. Miss Fluffernutter turned to address the now nearly empty auditorium. "Alrighty then! Anyone else? Last call for auditions!"

Miss Fluffernutter noticed Grace and asked, "Grace, are you sure you don't want to give it a shot?"

Charlotte chuckled. "You're barking up the wrong tree, Miss Fluffernutter. If there isn't a ball involved, it isn't for Grace."

Grace looked at her friend, all poised and pretty and perfect. She looked down at her own grass-stained trainers (that's "sneakers" to you!) and frayed jeans.

"It's just not her thing," Charlotte continued. "There's not enough dirt and sweat involved!"

Grace rubbed at a speck of dried mud on her knee.

"It's like I've been saying. Some people just don't appreciate the—"

"Okay, Miss Fluffernutter." Grace stood up. "I'm in."

Charlotte, Binah, Amy, and Nicole stared in openmouthed astonishment as Grace took the stage. She plugged her MP3 player into a set of speakers, and a beautiful melody filled the air. Grace turned and began to sing.

"True love . . ." she sang. Her voice was clear and pure. "You're the one I'm dreaming of . . ." *Where had Grace learned to sing like that?* Charlotte thought. "Your heart fits me like a glove . . ." Her voice soared. "True blue, baby, I love you." The final note hovered in the air as Grace jogged down the steps and back to her seat.

"C'mon, guys." She turned to her gape-mouthed friends. "Let's go home."

"GRACIE!" Amy shrieked. "Your voice is absolutely divine!!!"

"Yeah, where did you get those pipes, Grace?" Nicole asked, raising her head from a flurry of note taking.

"Oh, I don't know," Grace said with a wave of her hand. "I've always just liked singing along with music. I guess I get it from my mom. I even sing during practice sometimes."

Charlotte stared at the floor as jealousy welled up in her like a storm. She tried to push it back down, but the best she could do was mumble, "Nice job."

CHAPTER 6

The Best Juliet
You've Ever Seen

C'mon!!!

On Monday morning, Charlotte dragged the English Roses to school as fast as she could. Miss Fluffernutter was to post the cast list in the front hallway for everyone to see. Charlotte and Emma had spent all weekend practicing her "Juliet-isms," and she couldn't wait to show them off.

When they arrived, a large group had already formed inside the front doors. Charlotte sprinted ahead. She edged through the crowd, eyes on the prize. Students eased out of her way until she reached the list on the wall. Neck craning, she looked up at the column of names. She scanned them quickly until her eyes alighted on: "Romeo— William Worthington." Charlotte couldn't suppress a smile. She quickly scanned the rest of the list to find her own name. And then she saw it:

"Juliet Understudy—Charlotte Ginsberg."

"Congrats, Harrison!" William Worthington's familiar voice was unaccompanied by its usual hair-tug. Charlotte whipped around. Grace stood before her.

"What?" Grace asked. "Congrats on what?"

Charlotte felt hot tears prickling behind her eyes. Her throat felt tight and her hands clammy. She straightened her shoulders and looked at her friend. "Well, on this, of course." She pointed to the list, right above her own name. "You're Juliet. I'm very happy for you." And before the tears overflowed and spilled down her cheeks, she turned and quickly walked away.

When that morning's class began, Grace tried unsuccessfully to catch the eye of her friend. "Psst! Charlie!" But Charlotte sat stoically, staring at the blackboard ahead. Grace beaned her with an eraser. Nothing. A paper clip. Nothing still. She motioned to William to give her hair a tug. He obliged. Charlotte simply brushed her locks forward over her shoulders and did not turn around. Exasperated, Grace leaned over.

...the
BIG
BRUSH
OFF...

"Charlie, come *on*. I didn't even really audition! I just did it as a goof. I don't want the stupid part."

Charlotte bristled. "Well, you have it. And it certainly isn't stupid."

"I didn't mean it like that. I'm just saying, I'm not doing it. I don't know anything about theater."

Charlotte finally turned. "Well, that's true. And you really can't act."

Grace paused for a moment, mildly insulted. "Well, yeah. I mean . . ."

"And you don't have any experience performing." Grace started to object, but Charlotte barreled on.

"So you're right, it probably is best if you drop out. I mean, you wouldn't want to embarrass yourself."

Grace stared at her, her mouth open. Mrs. Moss cleared her throat.

"Girls? I'm sure you're all excited about the sixth-grade play, but—"

Grace suddenly stood. "I am, Mrs. Moss! And I'm going to be the best Juliet you've ever seen!"

Charlotte gasped. William Worthington exclaimed, "Right on!"

Mrs. Moss cocked her head. "I appreciate your spirit, Grace. And congratulations. But let's keep extracurricular activities just that: *extra-curricular*. Now, class. If you'll open your books to chapter two . . ."

BUMMER.

Charlotte looked down at her lap. This was going to be a long, long day.

She couldn't concentrate on a thing for the rest of the morning. Of course, her friends noticed (as best friends always do) and did their best to make her smile.

"Cheer up, Charlie!" Amy linked arms with her friend as they walked through the hall between classes. Binah joined them.

"Right," she agreed, smiling encouragingly. "Papa always says, 'Everything happens for a reason.'"

"Besides," piped in Nicole, "you're as close to the lead as it gets! Don't underestimate the understudy. You never know when you might have to fill in."

Charlotte smiled weakly. She appreciated everyone's efforts, but it was no use. She eyed Grace, waiting for the girls at the end of the hallway. Grace waved. Charlotte turned to her friends.

"You go on to class without me," she said, swallowing hard. "I'll meet you there." And before they could protest, she ducked into an alcove, then ran and slipped into her seat just before the bell rang so she didn't have to talk to anyone else.

Arriving home that afternoon, Charlotte shuffled up the long curving drive, dragging her feet and staring glumly at the ground. She heaved a sigh as she threw open the front door.

The phone was ringing as she entered her room. Falling backward onto her bed, she answered listlessly. "Hello?"

"Charlie! Oh good, you're there. Listen, I'm so, so, *so* sorry." Grace waited a beat for her friend to reply. "Charlie? Hello?"

"I'm here," said Charlotte. She blinked back tears. "I'm sorry, too! I don't even know what I was saying today. Of course you deserve the part." Charlotte tried extremely hard to believe what she was saying. She knew it was what a real friend would think. But then, why was it so hard for *her?*

Grace sounded beyond relieved. "Really? Oh, thank you thank you thank you! It means a lot to hear you say that."

Charlotte buried her head in her hands. If she could possibly have felt any worse, that did it.

"Charlie, there's no way I can do this without you. You have to help me!" Grace pleaded. "You're, like, a professional actress. I have no idea what I'm doing. Say you'll teach me. Please? Please, please, please, please, please . . ."

"Okay, okay!" Charlotte agreed. "Come over tomorrow after school and we'll get started."

"Thankyouthankyouthankyou! You're the best, Charlie."

"See you tomorrow, Gracie."

"'Kay. Bye!"

Charlotte placed the phone back on the receiver and buried her face in a fluffy feather pillow. Grace was one of her best friends. She needed to be there for her, even if it was the hardest thing she'd ever done. Which, Charlotte suspected, it would more than likely be.

Charlotte was
secretly
lonely in HER
"PALACE"
{shhhh....it's a "secret"}
don't TELL!!!

Friends are there to catch you when you fall.

CHAPTER 7

A Little Too Much of a Good Thing

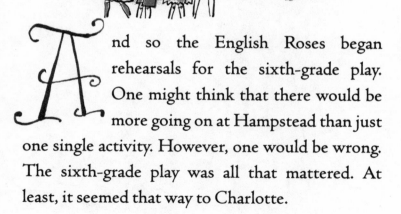

A nd so the English Roses began rehearsals for the sixth-grade play. One might think that there would be more going on at Hampstead than just one single activity. However, one would be wrong. The sixth-grade play was all that mattered. At least, it seemed that way to Charlotte.

Amy was working with a group of students to create costumes for the whole cast. They gathered

we ♡ sewing...

in the home ec room almost every afternoon to sew lace on velvet, stitch pockets onto flowing skirts, knit knickers onto knee socks. It was a lot of work, to be sure, but Amy loved every minute of it.

Binah had become a top-notch set designer. She couldn't describe how amazing it was to see buildings spring to life from *her* designs! Miss Fluffernutter had appointed an entire crew (mostly boys!) to help her. Binah was rather quiet by nature, but she was having a grand time telling the boys what to do!

Nicole, as expected, was running the show like a pro. Her prized possession was a headset walkie-talkie that she wore at all times to keep up with the goings-on backstage. Nicole *loved* that headset. She kept Miss Fluffernutter in line like a drill sergeant,

reminding her about rehearsal times and keeping her on task whenever her absentmindedness started to get the best of her.

William Worthington was actually turning out to be a rather talented Romeo. Except for the fact that when he was supposed to be under a balcony, he'd be perched in a tree. And when he ought to have been in a tree, he'd be under the balcony. But more often, when he was supposed to be in a tree, under a balcony, or anywhere else, instead he'd be out in the almost-empty auditorium, joking around with a certain someone who was watching from the dimly lit seats. Can you guess who that certain someone might be?

"Hey Charlie, wanna run lines with me?"

"Shh! I'm trying to listen."

"Bo-ring. Hey, did I tell you what Ashton said? It was hilarious. He was like—"

"William! Some of us actually care about the play. And aren't you supposed to be stage left? Nicole's going to kill you if she sees you over here."

"Uh-oh. Wouldn't want to get on Nicole's bad side. Yesterday after Alberto's solo she told him that he sounded like a dying elephant."

Charlotte unsuccessfully attempted to stifle a giggle. William grinned, triumphant. "So that's what it sounds like when you laugh! It's pretty nice. You should try it more often." Charlotte harumphed and swallowed a smile.

For her part, Charlotte had taken it upon herself to whip Grace into shape. It was a tough job, she thought, but someone had to do it. Every day after rehearsal, she and Grace would go back to her house and hole up in the studio for hours.

"Come on, Charlie. Can't we take a break? I'm tired!" Grace would whine. But Charlotte was no pushover.

"Real actresses don't take breaks," she would answer. And Grace would sigh and recite her lines all over again.

puff puff

"How was that, Charlie?" Grace would ask.

"Good, good," Charlotte would reply. "But . . . I think you can be better."

She knew she was being too tough, but Charlotte couldn't help it. If Grace was going to play Juliet—the part that was supposed to be HERS—she was going to have to do an extra-fantastic job!

A little enthusiasm is wonderful. But, as they say, too much of a good thing has a tendency to turn into anything but. As the air got colder and the days grew shorter, the English Roses seemed to be getting a little less rosy. One might even think that they were coming down with a case of "too much of a good thing" themselves.

1. eating: the play
2. sleeping: the play
3. breathing: the play

CHAPTER 8

True Love? I Think Not!

WILL WOULD
BE PROUD...

The English Roses saw less and less of one another as the days wore on. They missed one another dearly. Amy often found herself turning to relay some funny anecdote to Charlotte, only Charlotte wasn't there. Binah missed walking home with her friends—the night felt much colder

73

alone. Nicole even found that making lists wasn't nearly as pleasurable when Grace wasn't there to make fun of her for it. And Grace—well, Grace wasn't having much fun at all.

Charlotte was having a problem of her own. You see, at the end of *Romeo and Juliet: The Musical!*, there was a beautiful duet. Romeo and Juliet looked deep into each other's eyes and sang about how much they loved each other, and how their love would never die. And at the end of this song . . . they *kissed*.

Grace and William hadn't yet practiced the kiss onstage. But the end of the song was all Charlotte could think about. Grace was going to sing to William in her gorgeous, amazing angel's voice, and William was going to sing back, and they were

going to *kiss*. And Charlotte could hardly stand it.

The day before the show, Miss Fluffernutter made an announcement. They had never run the play the whole way through, so this afternoon was going to be a dress rehearsal.

Binah and her crew set the stage for the opening act. The cast scampered backstage to get into their costumes.

"All right, everybody—places, please!" Nicole instructed into her headset. In the back row, Charlotte tried to concentrate on the show. But all she could think about was that final duet. Grace and William . . . William and Grace . . . it was almost more than she could bear.

And then it was the final act. William stepped out onto the balcony, his hand over his heart. "More light and light, more dark and dark our woes!" He turned to Grace. "Farewell, farewell! One kiss and I'll descend."

Grace put her hand to his face. "No more sadness, I kiss it good-bye," she sang sweetly. "The sun is bursting right out of the sky." William took her hand.

"I searched the whole world for someone like you," he sang back.

"Don't you know, don't you know that it's *true love.* . . ." And slowly, slowly, they turned to look at each other. *"True love . . ."* They leaned in. *"True love . . ."* Closer still. Until finally—

"*Wait!*"

Everyone froze. Charlotte stood, her mouth open, hearing her own word echoing throughout the room. Charlotte felt the blood rush to her face; she knew she must be bright red. The silence in the auditorium was deafening. Then, from onstage, Grace cleared her throat.

"Right—absolutely, we should wait," she said. "I—I need to go. Practice. I need more practice."

William gave her a thumbs-up. "Right on, Harrison. Hey, I won't see you till tomorrow. So break a leg!"

"Right. Break a leg." She nodded. "See you tomorrow, then." And with that, she bolted from the stage.

CHAPTER 9

Isn't This Supposed to Be Fun?

DRAMA!

"Thanks for saving me there," said Grace. She was a little out of breath, Charlotte was walking so fast. Grace was usually the one in the lead, but tonight she could barely keep up. "Ew. Kissing William once is going to be bad enough. I don't exactly want to *practice* it, too!" Grace jogged to catch up with her speedy friend. "I mean, ick!"

HURRY... HURRY...

Charlotte nodded. "Ick is right." She looked at her watch. "Come on. It's getting late and we have a lot of work to do."

Grace eyed her friend. "Right. Okay then. Let's do it."

After what seemed like hours, Grace finally flopped to the floor, exhausted. "Can't I go home yet? I'm sooooo tired! If I keep this up I won't have any lungs left."

"Lungs schmungs!" scoffed Charlotte. "Again!"

Grace grimaced. "Charlie, I'm not kidding. I'm spent."

"Don't be a baby. Come on, again."

"Pleeeease?"

"Stop whining."

"Seriously. My knee is killing me. I think I bent it wrong or something when we were doing all those posture exercises."

"Your knee is fine."

"Ugh! Isn't this supposed to be *fun*?"

Charlotte stopped. It *was* supposed to be fun. And this? This was anything *but*.

Grace looked up at her imploringly.

Charlotte heaved a sigh that seemed to come from deep inside her. "Oh, all right," she conceded. "We'll stop for tonight. But I want you to drink two bottles of water and go to bed immediately," she barked. "Hydration and rest are two of the most important parts of a successful performance."

Grace kissed her friend and ran out the door.

CHAPTER 10

Opening Night

"I think I may actually die of excitement! Can you die of excitement?" Amy implored Binah and Nicole, who stood with her in the brisk fall air outside of Hampstead School, waiting for the last two Roses to arrive. "Because if you can, I certainly might!"

It was *Opening Night*. Binah felt those had to be the two most important words ever in the history of the world. For about a week straight, she'd relished saying them every chance she got. It really has quite a ring to it, don't you think?

Amy looked at her watch. "Where *are* they?" Charlotte and Grace had not yet arrived, and that was very strange indeed. This morning Amy had gotten a ride early so she could put finishing touches on the costumes, and Binah had been tweaking the final details on her set pieces since the crack of dawn. Nicole said she had so much to organize that walking with her friends would have been too distracting.

Binah rationalized the delay. "They were probably up late practicing. I'm sure Grace slept over and they just got a late start." She paused for a moment. "Though I don't know how they could have slept at all, right before Opening Night!"

"Hey, girls! Sorry I'm late." There was Charlotte, rounding the corner. "Were you waiting long?"

waiting...

"We've been waiting *forever!*" Amy exclaimed.

"Where's Grace?" asked Nicole.

Charlotte shrugged. "I thought she'd be here with you."

"She didn't sleep over at your house?" asked Binah.

"Nope." Charlotte shook her head. "What time is it? I'm sure she's on her way."

Riiiiing! The bell rang. A look of panic flashed across Nicole's face.

"We have to go in! We'll be late!" The girls exchanged glances.

"I'm sure she'll be here in a minute," Charlotte reasoned. "Let's just go in. No sense in all of us getting tardies."

Amy gave one last look down the street. No

Grace. "Okay, I guess," she reluctantly agreed.

The second bell rang with a blast. "C'mon," Charlotte urged. "Let's go." The Roses turned and followed her inside.

"Please take your seats, everyone," Mrs. Moss announced, looking down her nose at four out of five Roses. "I know it's a big night for all of you, but school is school. And there will be no dillydallying just because it's Opening Night." The words sent their usual thrill through Binah. "Now that we're all here," Mrs. Moss continued—then stopped. She cocked her head, scanning the room. "One, two, three, four . . . Girls, where's Grace?" Nicole, Binah, Amy, and Charlotte glanced at one another. *Good question*, they all thought.

Just then the classroom door opened. All heads

turned to the back of the class. And the students let out a huge gaping gasp that sucked the air right out of the room. If you've ever seen a hot-air balloon deflate, or stuck a fork into a marshmallow you've just taken out of the microwave, then you might have some small inkling of what it felt like to be in Mrs. Moss's classroom when Grace opened the door to come in late on the morning of Opening Night.

CHAPTER II

"Break a Leg" Is Just a Saying

"G race!" Mrs. Moss exclaimed. "What happened to you?" For there Grace stood, leaning against the doorway, supported by a pair of crutches.

"Gracie!" Amy yelped, leaping to her feet. "What on earth . . ." Nicole cut her off, running to help Grace into the room. "Are you all right?"

"I'll take your bag!" insisted Binah. "Here, grab my hand!"

"Jeez, Harrison," William Worthington piped in. "When I said 'break a leg,' I didn't mean it literally!"

"It's okay; I'm fine, really," Grace protested as

she hobbled to her seat. "Don't worry about me." Binah held Grace's crutches as she lowered herself into her chair.

"Grace, what happened to your leg?" asked Mrs. Moss.

"I must have pulled something," Grace admitted. "During rehearsal." The room grew quiet. She was probably overreacting, but Charlotte had the distinct feeling that all eyes were suddenly on her.

"It's not so bad," Grace continued. "It really only hurts when I . . . well . . . walk."

Nicole swallowed.

"Or stand."

Binah bit her lip.

"Or move. Like, at all."

Amy looked down.

"The doctor says it should be fine soon. But . . ." And here Grace's voice faltered a bit. "I . . . um . . . I won't be able to do the play."

Did I say all the air had already been sucked out of the room? Well, there must have been some left, because upon hearing these words, Mrs. Moss's class deflated even more. Charlotte almost couldn't breathe.

"I'm very sorry, Grace," Mrs. Moss said quietly. "I know how excited you were about the show. And you've certainly worked very hard." She glanced at Grace's bandaged knee. "A little too hard, from the look of it."

"Yeah. I guess so," said Grace.

"I know it will be difficult to focus, class," said Mrs. Moss. "But we must carry on. Because, unfortunately, learning doesn't take a holiday, even for pulled knees." She walked to her desk and took out her notes. "Now, on to last night's assignment. Who has thoughts on chapter five that they'd like to share?"

The students slowly settled back into their seats. But Charlotte sat stock-still, unable to lift her hands to pull back the curtain of hair that had fallen into her face. She felt a gentle tap on her shoulder, but couldn't find the strength to turn around.

"Hey." She felt William leaning close behind her. But it didn't sound like him. At least, it didn't sound like the William Worthington who pulled her hair and called her Charlie and got her into trouble with Mrs. Moss pretty much every day.

"Hey, Charlotte," William whispered. She didn't think he'd ever said her whole name before. "Don't worry. She's gonna be okay." And at that moment, Charlotte had never felt more like crying in her whole entire life.

The end of the day finally arrived. The double doors at the end of the hallway beckoned to Charlotte. This had truly been the longest day of her life.

"Charlie! Where are you going?" Amy rounded the corner, her arms full of beautiful velvet-and-lace bustled gowns. "Come on. We still have so much to do!"

Binah appeared behind her. "Yeah—only a few hours to go!" Charlotte kept walking.

"Come on, we have a lot to go over," Nicole said insistently, tapping her fingers nervously against her headset. She tugged Charlotte's arm. "Are you okay?"

"I'm going home," said Charlotte quietly. The Roses stared back at her, speechless.

"What's wrong with you?" Amy asked.

"It's over. Grace can't go on." She couldn't figure out why everyone was looking at her like she was crazy. What didn't they understand? "Show's over, girls. There can't be Romeo and Juliet when Juliet can't be in the play." *And Juliet isn't in the play because of me*, she finished to herself silently.

"But Juliet *will* be in the play," came a voice from behind her. She turned around. Grace met her eyes.

"We don't have a Juliet," Charlotte said. Had Grace hit her head as well as her knee? What didn't she understand?

"Yes, we do," Grace countered. "You."

"Parting is such sweet sorrow, that I shall say good night till it be morrow."

CHAPTER 12

Snap Out of It

can U see the forest for the trees?

Have you ever heard the expression She couldn't see the forest for the trees? For as Charlotte stood backstage with her friends as they readied themselves for the biggest night of their lives, she was suddenly faced with something that should have been the most obvious thing in the world. While to everyone else it was quite clear that she was Grace's understudy—she would be the one to go on if Grace couldn't—for some reason that thought had never entered Charlotte's head. She'd been working with Grace for weeks; she'd been going to rehearsals every single night; she'd been thinking about nothing but the sixth-grade play day in and day out. Yet she had not once thought about the fact that she was Grace's understudy.

"You guys!" she suddenly cried, wrenched from her reverie. "You guys . . . I don't know my lines!"

Well, the English Roses were certainly in a pickle. They looked to Nicole, who always had an answer

attention: this is
one
PIC
KLe.

for everything. But she just stood frozen, her mouth forming a tiny *o*.

"Should I get Miss Fluffernutter?" Binah finally asked. "We should probably tell her we have to . . . cancel the play." Binah had never uttered more heartbreaking words.

Amy blinked back tears. "I suppose so," she said.

Charlotte thought she'd felt terrible before, but this was the *worst*. She didn't think she'd ever recover.

"I'm so, so sorry," she said. "This is all my fault." And then, in a rush, tears she'd been holding back all day could no longer be contained. They filled her eyes and spilled over her cheeks. She took a jagged breath and then, along with her tears, words came pouring out in a torrent of sobs.

Waaaaaaa hhhhh!!!

"I was so jealous of you, Grace!" she wailed. "I made you work too hard! I never learned my lines! I'm the whole reason you hurt your knee, and now you can't go on, and the play is ruined, and it's all my fault!" Her shoulders shook. "Everything is *all my fault!*"

Amy, Binah, and Nicole threw their arms around her. "It's okay," they said. "Don't cry. Please don't cry." But Charlotte didn't think she'd ever be able to stop.

"Snap out of it!" Grace said.

Charlotte hiccupped, and the girls turned to face their incapacitated friend. "This isn't in the spirit of the theater!" Grace held one of her crutches in the air and shook it for emphasis. "I did *not* go through a zillion hours of practice, miss tons of sports time, not to mention *kiss William Worthington*"—she shuddered—"well, *almost* kiss William Worthington—to let it all go down like this. I'd expect more of you. Especially you." She turned to the sniffling Charlotte. "So you let a little jealousy get in your way. Don't let it destroy everything you love. You *love* the theater, Charlotte. More than anyone. And you just wanted me to be the best Juliet I could be." She turned back to the rest of the Roses. "So pull yourselves together! If there's one thing I've learned from all of this drama stuff, it's that *the show must go on!*"

The girls stared at her. She grinned. "Now are we going to get Shakespearian or what? Because I have a *plan!*"

CHAPTER 13

A Small Problem

The curtain parted. If you hadn't been
sitting in a packed auditorium with a
program in your hand expecting to see
some Shakespeare, you would have
sworn you were in the streets of Italy, so realistic and
well designed were the sets. Before he could remember himself, Binah's father leapt to his feet. "Bravo!"

he cheered. Polite giggles fluttered around him. Blushing, he lowered himself back into his seat. He just couldn't help himself—he was so proud of his daughter!

Backstage, the English Roses huddled together. Charlotte paced rapidly back and forth. "I can't! I can't do this," she protested.

Binah made the SETS

"Nonsense!" Nicole rebuffed her. "You can do this, Charlie," she said reassuringly. "If anyone can, it's you."

"That's right," Amy agreed. She was on her hands and knees, speedily sewing a tiny pocket onto the underside of the magnificent deep red velvet dress she'd helped Charlotte into moments earlier. "And you look absolutely gorgeous."

"Do I?" Charlotte tried to steal a glimpse of herself, but there was nary a mirror to be found. "Ouch!"

"Sorry!" Amy said, sheepishly holding the offending needle.

Charlotte's hands flew to her head. "I haven't even had time to warm up. And my hair—"

"Your hair is fine!" Grace hobbled over. "Now, here's the deal." She held out her hands. In one lay her mobile phone (mō·bīl phone: a British term for cell phone) and in the other her ever-present earphones. She plugged the earphones into the phone, then reached up and inserted one bud into Charlotte's ear. "Now this . . . goes in here," she said, threading the wire underneath the bodice of Charlotte's dress and slipping the phone into the newly stitched skirt pocket underneath.

"Perfect!" she exclaimed. Grace took a different mobile phone from Nicole. She dialed quickly. Suddenly, Charlotte's dress started ringing!

"Go ahead, answer it!" Grace urged. Charlotte reached into the pocket and activated the phone.

"Can you hear me?" Grace said into her own

phone, gesturing to the headphone in Charlotte's ear. Charlotte nodded. Grace smoothed Charlotte's long, dark hair over her ear to hide the device. She looked into her friend's eyes and smiled.

"Perfect," she said into her phone. "Romeo, Romeo . . ."

Charlotte nodded, understanding. Grace would feed her the lines over the phone. She'd hear them in her earphones and then broadcast them out loud as Juliet for the audience to hear.

(all together now....)

"wherefore art thou

Romeo?""

". . . Wherefore art thou, Romeo?" she and Grace finished in unison. Charlotte took Grace's hand and squeezed it tight.

"Oh, Gracie!" she said. "I can't thank you enough. But how is your knee? Does it hurt? I feel so terrible—"

"My knee is fine. No time to worry about that! Now, go get 'em, Juliet," she replied.

Nicole put her arms around them both. "Okay, Charlie. You're on." Charlotte looked at her friends' eager and encouraging faces. And suddenly, all her fear and self-doubt evaporated. It was as simple as that. They believed in her, so she would believe in herself.

"Okay," she said. "Let's do this!"

Charlotte stepped onto the stage. The audience burst into applause. She looked truly radiant in the gorgeous costume. With the support of her friends and Grace's guiding voice in her ear, Charlotte brought Juliet's words to life.

With each line, her confidence blossomed. And soon it became clear that all the hours she'd spent coaching Grace had helped the words take root within herself as well. For as she spoke, she realized she no longer had to wait for Grace to feed her the line; she already knew what she was supposed to say. She had really known it all along. As her talent overcame her nerves, she found herself in love with performing more than ever before.

It was time for the first song. Charlotte turned to find William—her Romeo—watching her from the other side of the stage. The music piped in for their opening duet. William sang his first line with a sparkle in his eye. His voice rang out clear and true, and Charlotte almost swooned as he sang to her. He really was quite a good actor, she had to admit. Imagine, being inspired to feel anything but annoyed at William Worthington!

William finished his opening stanza. He looked expectantly at Charlotte, who was to sing back her reply. The music swelled. Charlotte opened her mouth. There was just one teeny, tiny, little problem.

Charlotte couldn't sing.

It's a teeny tiny itsy bitsy small small small SMALL PROBLEM...

CHAPTER 14

Willy-Nilly Kisses

Now, that's not altogether fair. Charlotte could sing. Charlotte just couldn't sing very well. Under ordinary circumstances, she wasn't terrible. But there, center stage, under the hot white lights with a sea of faces staring up at her, her voice got tangled up in itself and caught in her throat. And what came out of her mouth was less of a note than a squeak. Or, more accurately, a screech. The audience actually winced. William took a step back. Grace was so stunned she forgot to feed the words into the phone for Charlotte to sing out loud. So what choice did Charlotte have but to hold one, long, extended note until Grace recovered and could help her through the rest of the song? Amy grabbed Grace's arm.

"We have to do something!" Unfortunately, Grace was out of ideas.

Suddenly Nicole jumped to her feet. "Here! Take this," she said, grabbing her beloved headset off her own head and fixing it onto Grace's. She pulled the cord out of the microphone pack on her waist and turned to Grace. "On my signal," she instructed, "you're going to sing." And with that she sprinted off, leaving Binah, Amy, and Grace staring after her.

"What signal?" Grace finally asked, dazed.

"Sing!" Nicole's urgent whisper came from the headset's earpiece as if on cue.

Out in the audience, a low murmur rumbled through the seats as Charlotte's painful screeching continued. Her eyes were growing desperate; she wasn't sure how much longer she could go without taking a breath! From the look of it, William

Worthington wasn't sure how much longer *he* could go without holding his *ears*.

"Sing!" came Nicole's whisper again. Amy and Binah gestured at Grace. *Do it!* She took a deep breath, angled the headset microphone just so . . .

. . . and began to sing.

A clear and beautiful voice echoed from speakers above the stage. Charlotte trailed off as Grace's

perfect song floated over the crowd. Binah and Amy high-fived each other and Nicole smiled proudly at her accomplishment, the headset cord now plugged into the auditorium speakers so that Grace's singing could be broadcast out loud to the crowd. And no one was happier than Charlotte, who beamed as Grace's song of love wrapped Romeo and Juliet in an invisible embrace.

The rest of the play went by in a flash. Charlotte felt it was almost over just as soon as it began. For suddenly she found herself standing on a balcony, locked in William's gaze, as the last notes of the last song drifted away.

The final duet now but a memory, William turned to Charlotte and held out his hand. "*True love . . .*"

This is it, thought Charlotte. *This is the kiss!* Her breath quickened. William leaned in. Charlotte leaned in. William closed his eyes. Charlotte closed hers. And slowly, gently, she reached forward . . . and smooched him on the cheek!

William started in surprise. His eyes popped open, and Charlotte's met them with a wink. She had come to the realization that she was a little confused about her feelings for William Worthington. And Charlotte Ginsberg was not one to go around kissing boys willy-nilly, even when they were quite cute with flashing blue-green eyes. No indeed; her lips were off-limits for the time being. William grinned at her. And it looked as if he just might be willing to wait!

When the final curtain closed, the roar of the audience was almost deafening! The crowd rose to its feet. "Bravo!" cried Emma from her seat in the front row. Charlotte's mother looked beautiful in a satin ballgown as she clutched her husband's tuxedoed arm. They beamed at each other, so proud of their talented daughter. Binah's father was relieved to be able to cheer as loudly as he liked. Miss Fluffernutter motioned for the cast to join her onstage. They took a bow, and Charlotte let the praise wash over her. She'd never felt anything like it! It was the greatest feeling ever. Next to her,

William reached over and took her hand. She turned to him, startled. He just shrugged, and smiled, and lifted her hand into the air with his. *Scratch that*, Charlotte thought. *Now* this *is the best feeling ever!*

Charlotte glanced into the wings where the rest of the Roses beamed at her and applauded wildly. She gestured for them to join her. Amy grinned and bounded right out to meet her. Binah shyly followed but lost all self-consciousness when she caught sight of her father cheering her on. Nicole smiled as Miss Fluffernutter swept her up into a huge bear hug. "I could never have done this without you!" she thanked her.

Charlotte locked eyes with Grace, still standing in the wings. She held her arms out, opened wide.

Grace laughed and came over to her, and the girls embraced in the kind of hug only truly great friends can share.

Suddenly, a huge bouquet of red roses was thrust between them. William stood grinning, his arms full of flowers.

"Sorry to interrupt," he said, handing Charlotte the bouquet. "But here, Charlie. These are for you." Charlotte stared down at the flowers, speechless. William shrugged. "You did a pretty okay job there. Not as good as *I*, but still." Say what you will about William Worthington; his grammar was impeccable!

"Thanks," Charlotte said, admiring the beautiful blooms. "But I think these belong to someone else." She turned to Grace. "Here you go, Juliet," she said.

"Thanks, Juliet," Grace said, accepting the bouquet.

The two girls burst into giggles and clasped hands. Binah, Amy, and Nicole ran down to join them. And as the audience continued to cheer, they took one final bow together, knowing they would never ever forget this most incredible sixth-grade play.

It was only when the cast and crew filed off the stage to meet friends and parents out in the lobby that Charlotte noticed something. Walking across the empty stage, her eyes fell on a most puzzling sight. For there, lying forgotten among the discarded props and costumes littering the backstage area, was a single pair of crutches.

CHAPTER 15

That's What Friends Are For

That night, the English Roses gathered at Charlotte's house for a post-play sleep-over. Winston brought them Nigella's famous hot cocoa with tiny marshmallows and whipped cream, and extra fudgy brownies with huge chocolate chunks and buttery pink icing. Exhausted, they all piled into sleeping bags. As they

snuggled in for the night and began to drop off to sleep, Charlotte piped up.

"Thank you all so much for everything."

"Nothing to thank us for," said the dozing Nicole. The others murmured in agreement.

"Really," Charlotte whispered to Grace. "I couldn't have done it without you."

"You were great, Charlie," said Grace. "It should have been you all along."

"But you worked so hard." Charlotte turned to her friend. Grace was almost buried under a pile of pillows. "I'm really, really sorry, Gracie," she whispered. "I should never have let my stupid jealousy keep me from being your friend. That's more important than anything. And I feel so terrible about your knee!"

"Thank you. But my knee really didn't hurt THAT bad." Grace smiled. "And you were the one who worked hard," she admitted. "I was just trying to keep up. You were born to be Juliet. Besides"—she burrowed farther into the pile of down—

"performing in front of *all those people*?!? I'm not brave enough for that. You're the star, Charlotte."

Charlotte paused. She thought of the abandoned crutches backstage, and how Grace had had no trouble bounding up the stairs to her room when they came up to bed.

"But . . . Grace," she said softly, "the crutches. I saw you run onto the stage without them."

"Well, um, I guess your performance restored my knee to its former ferocious state," Grace giggled.

"Thank you, Grace. I couldn't ask for a better friend than you!" Charlotte said, squeezing her friend's hand.

Grace yawned. "Hey, Mrs. Moss said we could start an indoor football team this winter! Now that the play is over, you wanna join?"

"Sure!" Charlotte said. "As long as I can be a cheerleader!"

The girls laughed. It truly is a wonderful thing to have a best friend. And just imagine having *four* of them! Charlotte knew she was very lucky indeed. And with that the English Roses drifted off to sleep, knowing that whatever adventures life had in store for them, they could do anything. As long as they did it together.

The End

MADONNA RITCHIE was born in Bay City, Michigan, and now lives in London and Los Angeles with her husband, movie director Guy Ritchie, and her children, Lola, Rocco, and David. She has recorded 17 albums and appeared in 18 movies. This is the third in her series of chapter books. She has also written six picture books for children, starting with the international bestseller *The English Roses*, which was released in 40 languages and more than 100 countries.

PICTURE BOOKS:

The English Roses
Mr. Peabody's Apples
Yakov and the Seven Thieves
The Adventures of Abdi
Lotsa de Casha
The English Roses: Too Good To Be True

CHAPTER BOOKS:

Friends For Life!
Good-Bye, Grace?
The New Girl

JEFFREY FULVIMARI was born in Akron, Ohio. He started coloring when he was two, and has never stopped. Soon after graduating from The Cooper Union in New York City, he began drawing for magazines and television commercials around the globe. He currently lives in a log cabin in upstate New York, and is happiest when surrounded by stacks of paper and magic markers.